Eurydice

by
Sarah Ruhl

A SAMUEL FRENCH ACTING EDITION

SAMUEL FRENCH

FOUNDED 1830

NEW YORK HOLLYWOOD LONDON TORONTO

SAMUELFRENCH.COM

IMPORTANT BILLING AND CREDIT REQUIREMENTS

All producers of *EURYDICE* *must* give credit to the Author of the Play in all programs distributed in connection with performances of the Play, and in all instances in which the title of the Play appears for the purposes of advertising, publicizing or otherwise exploiting the Play and/or a production. The name of the Author *must* appear on a separate line on which no other name appears, immediately following the title and *must* appear in size of type not less than fifty percent of the size of the title type.

a.) Playwright shall receive billing credit as the sole Author of the Play whenever and wherever the title of the Play appears as follows:

EURYDICE

by

Sarah Ruhl

No one shall receive larger or more prominent billing than the billing accorded Playwright hereunder. Playwright's name shall be in at least fifty percent (50%) size, type, and prominence of the title of the Play and said billing shall appear in all programs, posters, house boards, circulars, advertising, and announcements of The Play under Producer's management or control.

b.) Producer agrees to provide the following billing on the title page of the program. No inadvertent failure to accord the billing herein provided shall be deemed a breach hereof so long as same is corrected as soon as practicable after notice.

"This play was originally produced by Madison Repertory Theatre, Madison, Wisconsin, August 29, 2003. Richard Corley, Artistic Director, Tony Forman, Managing Director.

And subsequently produced by Berkeley Repertory Theatre in 2004. Tony Taccone, Artistic Director, Susan Medak, Managing Director. And Yale Repertory Theatre, James Bundy, Artistic Director, Victoria Nolan, Managing Director."

"Produced by Second Stage Theatre, New York, 2007 Carole Rothman: Artistic Director"

The size and prominence of the credits shall be not less than fifty percent (50%) of the largest of the credits given to any producer.

EURYDICE received its world premiere at Madison Repertory Theatre (Richard Corley, Artistic Director; Tony Forman, Managing Director) in September, 2003. The production was directed by Richard Corley; the set design was by Narelle Sissons, the lighting design was by Rand Ryan, the costume design was by Murell Horton, the sound design was by Darron L. West, and movement was by Karen Hoyer; the stage manager was Lynn Terry. The cast was as follows

EURYDICE . . . . Laura Heisler

HER FATHER . . . . John Lenertz

ORPHEUS . . . . David ANdrew McMahon

A NASTY INTERESTING MAN . . . . Scot Morton

GRANDMOTHER . . . . Diane Dorsey

BIG STONE . . . . Jody REiss

LITTLE STONE . . . . Polly Noonan

LOUD STONE . . . . Karlie Nurse

EURYDICE premiered on September 22, 2006 at the Yale Repertory Theatre (James Bundy, artistic director; Victoria Nolan, managing director). The production was directed by Les Waters, and featured choreography by John Carrafa, scenic design by Scott Bradley, costume design by Meg Neville, lighting design by Russell H. Champa, and sound design by Bray Poor. Amy Boratko was the dramaturg and James Mountcastle was the production stage manager. The cast was as follows:

EURYDICE. . . . . Maria Dizzia

LOUD STONE . . . . Gian-Murray Gianino

LITTLE STONE. . . . . Carla Harting

BIG STONE. . . . . Ramiz Monsef

ORPHEUS . . . . Joseph Parks

EURYDICE'S FATHER . . . . Charles Shaw Robinson

NASTY INTERESTING MAN/LORD OF THE UNDERWORLD Mark Zeisler

EURYDICE opened on June 18, 2007 at Second Stage Theatre. The production was directed by Les Waters, and featured choreography by John Carrafa, scenic design by Scott Bradley, costume design by Meg Neville, lighting design by Russell H. Champa, and sound design by Bray Poor.

EURYDICE. . . . . Maria Dizzia

LOUD STONE . . . . Gian-Murray Gianino

LITTLE STONE. . . . . Carla Harting

BIG STONE. . . . . Ramiz Monsef

ORPHEUS . . . . Joseph Parks

EURYDICE'S FATHER . . . . Charles Shaw Robinson

NASTY INTERESTING MAN/LORD OF THE UNDERWORLD Mark Zeisler

CHARACTERS

Eurydice
Her Father
Orpheus
A Nasty Interesting Man/The Lord of the Underworld

A Chorus of Stones:

> Big Stone
> Little Stone
> Loud Stone

SETTING

The set contains a raining elevator,
a water-pump,
some rusty exposed pipes,
an abstracted River of Forgetfulness,
an old-fashioned glow-in-the-dark globe.

NOTES

Eurydice and Orpheus should be played as though they are a little too young and a little too in love. They should resist the temptation to be "classical."

The underworld should resemble the world of Alice in Wonderland more than it resembles Hades.

The stones might be played as though they are nasty children at a birthday party.

When people compose letters in this play they needn't actually scribble them – they can speak directly to the audience.

The play should be performed without an intermission.

ACKNOWLEDGEMENTS

Thank you to Christopher Steele-Nicholson. Thank you to Rick Corley for doing the first production of the play, Susannah Melone for being the very first Eurydice, Laura Heisler for being the second, to Polly and to Carla for having the humility and dexterity to play both Eurydice and little stone, and Maria for following the play to three cities. Thanks to all the actors, designers and directors who contributed to this play along its path – Daniel Fish for his water bottles, Rebecca Brown and Darron West for their red door in the Jimmy Jingle, Davis McCallum for the grandmother retreating into a row of trees in the open air, Scott Bradley for the letters ascending into heaven, and Joyce Piven for the circus flights and the exit door. Thanks to Joe Pucci and David Konstan for the Latin and the Greek. Thank you to Chuck Mee for giving this play to Les Waters, and for his inspiration with the Greeks; to Kathleen Tolan for getting me through New York previews, and to the Tolan-Mee daughters for being the ideal audience. Thanks to Mac Wellman who read the first draft, and to Paula Vogel for reading all the subsequent ones. And thank you to Les Waters, for everything. Thank you to Mom, Kate, and Tony for coming to every production.

This play is for my father.

FIRST MOVEMENT

Scene 1

A young man – Orpheus –
and a young woman – Eurydice.
They wear swimming outfits from the 1950s.
Orpheus makes a sweeping gesture with his arm, indicat-
ing the sky.

EURYDICE. All those birds?

He nods.

EURYDICE. For me? Thank you.

They make a quarter turn and he makes a sweeping
gesture.
He makes a gesture of giving the sea to Eurydice.

EURYDICE. And – the sea! Now?

Orpheus opens his hands.

EURYDICE. It's mine already?

Orpheus nods.

EURYDICE. Wow.

They kiss. He indicates the sky.

EURYDICE. Surely not – surely not the sky and the stars too.

Orpheus nods.

EURYDICE. That's very generous.

Orpheus nods.

EURYDICE. Perhaps too generous?

Orpheus shakes his head.

EURYDICE. Thank you.

She crawls on top of him and kisses his eyes.

EURYDICE. What are you thinking about?

ORPHEUS. Music.

EURYDICE. How can you think about music? You either hear it or you don't.

ORPHEUS. I'm hearing it then.

EURYDICE. Oh.

(Pause.)

I read a book today.

ORPHEUS. Did you?

EURYDICE. Yes. It was very interesting.

ORPHEUS. That's good.

EURYDICE. Don't you want to know what it was about?

ORPHEUS. Of course.

EURYDICE. There were – stories – about people's lives – how some come out well – and others come out badly.

ORPHEUS. Do you love the book?

EURYDICE. Yes – I think so.

ORPHEUS. Why?

EURYDICE. It can be interesting to see if other people – like dead people who wrote books – agree or disagree with what you think.

ORPHEUS. Why?

EURYDICE. Because it makes you – a larger part of the human community. It had very interesting arguments.

ORPHEUS. Oh. And arguments that are interesting are good arguments?

EURYDICE. Well – yes.

ORPHEUS. I didn't know an argument should be interesting. I thought it should be right or wrong.

EURYDICE. Well, these particular arguments were very interesting.

ORPHEUS. Maybe you should make up your own thoughts. Instead of reading them in a book.

EURYDICE. I do. I do think up my own thoughts.

ORPHEUS. I know you do. I love how you love books. Don't be mad.

Pause.

ORPHEUS. I made up a song for you today.

EURYDICE. Did you!?

ORPHEUS. Yup. It's not *interesting* or *not* -interesting. It just – is.

EURYDICE. Will you sing it for me?

ORPHEUS. It has too many parts.

EURYDICE. Let's go in the water.

They start walking, arm in arm,
on extensive unseen boardwalks, towards the water.

ORPHEUS. Wait – remember this melody.

He hums a bar of melody.

EURYDICE. I'm bad at remembering melodies. Why don't you remember it?

ORPHEUS. I have eleven other ones in my head, making for a total of twelve.

You have it?

EURYDICE. Yes. I think so.

ORPHEUS. Let's hear it.

She sings the melody.
She misses a few notes.
She's not the best singer in the world.

ORPHEUS. Pretty good. The rhythm's a little off. Here – clap it out.

She claps.
He claps the rhythmic sequence for her.
She tries to imitate.
She is still off.

EURYDICE. Is that right?

ORPHEUS. We'll practice.

EURYDICE. I don't need to know about rhythm. I have my books.

ORPHEUS. Don't books have rhythm?

EURYDICE. Kind of. Let's go in the water.

ORPHEUS. Will you remember my melody under the water?

EURYDICE. Yes! I WILL ALWAYS REMEMBER YOUR MELODY! It will be imprinted on my heart like wax.

ORPHEUS. Thank you.

EURYDICE. You're welcome. When are you going to play me the whole song?

ORPHEUS. When I get twelve instruments.

EURYDICE. Where are you going to get twelve instruments?

ORPHEUS. I'm going to make each strand of your hair into an instrument. Your hair will stand on end as it plays my music and become a hair orchestra. It will fly you up into the sky.

EURYDICE. I don't know if I want to be an instrument.

ORPHEUS. Why?

EURYDICE. Won't I fall down when the song ends?

ORPHEUS. That's true. But the clouds will be so moved by your music that they will fill up with water until they become heavy and you'll sit on one and fall gently down to earth. How about that?

EURYDICE. Okay.

They gaze at each other.

ORPHEUS. It's settled then.

EURYDICE. What is?

ORPHEUS. Your hair will be my orchestra and – I love you.

EURYDICE. I love you too.

ORPHEUS. How will you remember?

EURYDICE. That I love you?

ORPHEUS. Yes.

EURYDICE. That's easy. I can't help it.

ORPHEUS. You never know. I'd better tie a string around your finger to remind you.

EURYDICE. Is there string at the ocean?

ORPHEUS. I always have string. In case I come upon a broken instrument.

He takes out a string from his pocket.
He takes her left hand.

ORPHEUS. This hand.

He wraps string deliberately around her fourth finger.

ORPHEUS. Is this too tight?

EURYDICE. No – it's fine.

ORPHEUS. There – now you'll remember.

EURYDICE. That's a very particular finger.

ORPHEUS. Yes.

EURYDICE. You're aware of that?

ORPHEUS. Yes.

EURYDICE. How aware?

ORPHEUS. Very aware.

EURYDICE. Orpheus – are we?

ORPHEUS. You tell me.

EURYDICE. Yes.

I think so.

ORPHEUS. You *think* so?

EURYDICE. I wasn't thinking.

I mean – Yes. Just: Yes.

ORPHEUS. Yes?

EURYDICE. Yes.

ORPHEUS. Yes!

EURYDICE. Yes!

ORPHEUS. May our lives be full of music!

Music.
He picks her up and throws her into the sky.

EURYDICE. Maybe you could also get me another ring – a gold one – to put over the string one. You know?

ORPHEUS. Whatever makes you happy. Do you still have my melody?

EURYDICE. It's right here.

> *She points to her temple.*
> *They look at each other. A silence.*

EURYDICE. What are you thinking about?

ORPHEUS. Music.

> *Her face falls.*

ORPHEUS. Just kidding. I was thinking about you. And music.

EURYDICE. Let's go in the water. I'll race you!

> *She puts on her swimming goggles.*

ORPHEUS. I'll race *you!*

EURYDICE. I'll race *you!*

ORPHEUS. I'll race *you!*

EURYDICE. I'll race *you!*

> *They race towards the water.*

Scene 2

The Father, dressed in a grey suit, reads from a letter.

FATHER. Dear Eurydice,

A letter for you on your wedding day.

There is no choice of any importance in life but the choosing of a beloved. I haven't met Orpheus, but he seems like a serious young man. I understand he's a musician.

(The father thinks – oh, dear.)

If I were to give a speech at your wedding I would start with one or two funny jokes and then I might offer some words of advice. I would say:

Cultivate the arts of dancing and small talk.

Everything in moderation.

Court the companionship and respect of dogs.

Grilling a fish or toasting bread without burning requires singleness of purpose, vigilance and steadfast watching.

Keep quiet about politics, but vote for the right man.

Take care to change the light bulbs.

Continue to give yourself to others because that's the ultimate satisfaction in life – to love, accept, honor and help others.

As for me, this is what it's like being dead: the atmosphere smells. And there are strange high pitched noises – like a tea kettle always boiling over. But it doesn't seem to bother anyone. And, for the most part, there is a pleasant atmosphere and you can work and socialize, much like at home. I'm working in the business world and it seems that, here, you can better see the far reaching consequences of your actions.

Also, I am one of the few dead people who still remembers how to read and write. That's a secret. If anyone finds out, they might dip me in the River again.

I write you letters. I don't know how to get them to
you.

Love,
Your father

He drops the letter as though into a mail-slot.
It falls on the ground.

Wedding music.
In the underworld, the father walks in a
straight line as though he is walking his daughter down
the aisle,

He is affectionate, then solemn, then glad, then solemn,
then amused, then solemn.

He looks at his imaginary daughter; he looks straight
ahead; he acknowledges the guests at the wedding; he
gets choked up; he looks at his daughter and smiles an
embarrassed smile for getting choked up.

He looks straight ahead, calm.
He walks.

Suddenly, he checks his watch.
He exits, in a hurry.

Scene 3

Eurydice, by a water-pump.
The noise of a party, from far off.

EURYDICE. I hate parties.

And a wedding party is the biggest party of all.

All the guests arrived and Orpheus is taking a shower.

He's always taking a shower when the guests arrive so he doesn't have to greet them.

Then I have to greet them.

A wedding is for daughters and fathers. The mothers all dress up, trying to look like young women. But a wedding is for a father and a daughter. They stop being married to each other on that day.

I always thought there would be more interesting people at my wedding.

She drinks water from the water pump.
The Nasty Interesting Man, wearing a trench coat, appears and sees Eurydice cupping her hands full of water.

MAN. Are you a homeless person?

EURYDICE. No.

MAN. Oh. I'm on my way to a party where there are really very interesting people. Would you like to join me?

EURYDICE. No. I just left my own party.

MAN. You were giving a party and you just – left?

EURYDICE. I was thirsty.

MAN. You must be a very interesting person, to leave your own party like that.

EURYDICE. Thank you.

MAN. You mustn't care at all what other people think of you. I always say that's a mark of a really interesting person, don't you?

EURYDICE. I guess.

MAN. So would you like to accompany me to this interesting affair?

EURYDICE. No, thank you. I just got married, you see.

MAN. Oh – lots of people do that.

EURYDICE. That's true – lots of people do.

MAN. What's your name?

EURYDICE. Eurydice.

He looks at her, hungry.

MAN. Eurydice.

EURYDICE. Good-bye, then.

MAN. Good-bye.

She exits. He sits by the water pump.
He notices a letter on the ground.
He picks it up and reads it.

MAN. (*to himself*) Dear Eurydice.

Musty dripping sounds.

Scene 4

*The father tries to remember how to do the jitterbug in the
underworld.*
He does the jitterbug with an imaginary partner.
He has fun.

Orpheus and Eurydice dance together at their wedding.
They are happy.
They have had some champagne.
They sing together.

ORPHEUS AND EURYDICE. Don't sit under the apple tree
with anyone else but me
anyone else but me
anyone else but me
no no no
Don't sit under the apple tree
with anyone else but me,
'til I come marching home...

On the other side of the stage,
the Father checks his watch.
He stops doing the jitterbug.
He exits, in a hurry.

EURYDICE. I'm warm; are you warm?

ORPHEUS. Yes!

EURYDICE. I'm going to get a drink of water.

ORPHEUS. Don't go.

EURYDICE. I'll be right back.

ORPHEUS. Promise?

EURYDICE. Yes.

ORPHEUS. I can't stand to let you out of my sight tonight.

EURYDICE. Silly goose.

They kiss.

Scene 5

Eurydice at the water pump,
getting a glass of water.
The Interesting Man appears.

EURYDICE. Oh – you're still here.

MAN. Yes. I forgot to tell you something. I have a letter. Addressed to Eurydice – that's you – from your father.

EURYDICE. That's not possible.

MAN. He wrote down some thoughts – for your wedding day.

EURYDICE. Let me see.

MAN. I left it at home. It got delivered to my elegant high-rise apartment by mistake.

EURYDICE. Why didn't you say so before?

MAN. You left in such a hurry.

EURYDICE. From my father?

MAN. Yes.

EURYDICE. You're sure?

MAN. Yes.

EURYDICE. I knew he'd send something!

MAN. It'll just take a moment. I live around the block. What an interesting dress you're wearing.

EURYDICE. Thank you.

Scene 6

Orpheus, from the water pump.

ORPHEUS. Eurydice?
Eurydice!

Scene 7

The sound of a door closing.
The Interesting Apartment – a giant loft space with no furniture.
Eurydice and the Man enter, panting.

MAN. Voila.

EURYDICE. You're very high up.

MAN. Yes. I am.

EURYDICE. I feel a little faint.

MAN. It'll pass.

EURYDICE. Have you ever thought about installing an elevator?

MAN. No. I prefer stairs. I think architecture is so interesting, don't you?

EURYDICE. Oh, yes. So, where's the letter?

MAN. But isn't this an interesting building?

EURYDICE. It's so – high up.

MAN. Yes.

EURYDICE. There's no one here. I thought you were having a party.

MAN. I like to celebrate things quietly. With a few other interesting people. Don't you?

She tilts her head to the side and stares at him.

Would you like some champagne?

EURYDICE. Maybe some water.

MAN. Water it is! Make yourself comfortable.

He gestures to the floor.
He switches on Brazilian mood music.
She looks around.

EURYDICE. I can't stay long!

She looks out the window. She is very high up.

EURYDICE. I can see my wedding from here!
The people are so small – they're dancing!

There's Orpheus!

He's not dancing.

MAN. (*Shouting from off-stage*) So, who's this guy you're marrying?

EURYDICE. (*shouting*) His name is Orpheus.

MAN. (*as he attempts to open the champagne, off-stage.*) Orpheus. Not a very interesting name. I've heard it before.

EURYDICE. (*shouting*) Maybe you've heard of him. He's kind of famous. He plays the most beautiful music in the world, actually.

MAN. I can't hear you!

EURYDICE. (*shouting*) So the letter was delivered – here – today?

MAN. That's right.

EURYDICE. Through the post?

MAN. It was – mysterious.

The sound of champagne popping.
He enters with one glass of champagne.

MAN. Voila.

He drinks the champagne.

So. Eurydice. Tell me one thing. Name me one person you find interesting.

EURYDICE. Why?

MAN. Just making conversation.

He sways a little, to the music.

EURYDICE. Right. Um – all the interesting people I know are dead or speak French.

MAN. Well, I don't speak French, Eurydice.

He takes one step toward her.
She takes one step back.

EURYDICE. I'm sorry. I have to go. There's no letter, is there?

MAN. Of course there's a letter. It's right here.

He pats his breast pocket.

MAN. Eurydice. I'm not interesting, but I'm strong. You could teach me to be interesting. I would listen. Orpheus is too busy listening to his own thoughts. There's music in his head. Try to pluck the music out and it bites you. I'll bet you had an interesting thought today, for instance.

She tilts her head to the side, quizzical.

I bet you're always having them, the way you tilt your head to the side and stare...

She jerks her head back up.
Musty dripping sounds.

EURYDICE. I feel dizzy all of a sudden. I want my husband. I think I'd better go now.

MAN. You're free to go, whenever you like.

EURYDICE. I know.

I think I'll go now, in fact. I'll just take my letter first, if you don't mind.

She holds out her hand for the letter.
He takes her hand.

MAN. Relax.

She takes her hand away.

EURYDICE. Good-bye.

She turns to exit.
He blocks the doorway.

MAN. Wait. Eurydice. Don't go. I love you.

EURYDICE. Oh no.

MAN. You need to get yourself a real man. A man with broad shoulders like me. Orpheus has long fingers that would tremble to pet a bull or pluck a bee from a hive –

EURYDICE. How do you know about my husband's fingers?

MAN. A man who can put his big arm around your little shoulders as he leads you through the crowd, a man who answers the door at parties.... A man with big hands, with big stupid hands like potatoes, a man who can carry a cow in labor.

The man backs Eurydice against the wall.

MAN. My lips were meant to kiss your eyelids, that's obvious!

EURYDICE. Close your eyes, then!

He closes his eyes, expecting a kiss.
She takes the letter from his breast pocket.
She slips under him and opens the door to the stairwell.
He opens his eyes.
She looks at the letter.

EURYDICE. It's his handwriting!

MAN. Of course it is!

He reaches for her.

EURYDICE. Good-bye.

She runs for the stairs.
She wavers, off-balance, at the top of the stairwell.

MAN. Don't do that, you'll trip!

EURYDICE. Orpheus!

From the water-pump:

ORPHEUS. EURYDICE!

She runs, trips and pitches down the stairs, holding her letter.
She follows the letter down, down down...
Blackout. A clatter. Strange sounds – xylophones, brass bands, sounds of falling, sounds of vertigo.
Sounds of breathing.

SECOND MOVEMENT

The underworld.
There is no set change.
Strange watery noises.
Drip, drip, drip.
The movement to the underworld is marked
by the entrance of stones.

Scene 1

THE STONES. We are a chorus of stones.

LITTLE STONE. I'm a little stone.

BIG STONE. I'm a big stone.

LOUD STONE. I'm a loud stone.

THE STONES. We are all three stones.

LITTLE STONE. We live with the dead people in the land of the dead.

BIG STONE. Eurydice was a great musician. Orpheus was his wife.

LOUD STONE. (*correcting Big Stone.*) Orpheus was a great musician. Eurydice was his wife. She died.

LITTLE STONE. Then he played the saddest music.
Even we –

THE STONES. The stones –

LITTLE STONE. Cried when we heard it.

The sound of three drops of water hitting a pond.

LITTLE STONE. Oh, look,
she is coming into the land of the dead now.

BIG STONE. Oh!

LOUD STONE. Oh!

LITTLE STONE. Oh!

We might say – "Poor Eurydice" –

LOUD STONE. But stones don't feel bad for
dead people.

The sound of an elevator ding.
An elevator door opens.
Inside the elevator, it is raining.
Eurydice gets rained on inside the elevator.
She carries a suitcase and an umbrella.
She is dressed in the kind of 1930s suit that women wore
when they eloped.
She looks bewildered.

The sound of an elevator ding.
Eurydice steps out of the elevator.
The elevator door closes.

She walks towards the audience and opens her mouth,
trying to speak.
There is a great humming noise.
She closes her mouth.
The humming noise stops.
She opens her mouth for the second time,
attempting to tell her story to the audience.
There is a great humming noise.
She closes her mouth – the humming noise stops.
She has a tantrum of despair.

STONES. Eurydice wants to speak to you.

But she can't speak your language anymore.

She talks in the language of dead people now.

LITTLE STONE. It's a very quiet language.

LOUD STONE. Like if the pores in your face
opened up and talked.

BIG STONE. Like potatoes sleeping in the dirt.

The stones look at Big Stone as though that were a dumb
thing to say.

LITTLE STONE. Pretend that you understand her
    or she'll be embarrassed.

BIG STONE. Yes – pretend for a moment
    that you understand
    the language of stones.

LOUD STONE. Listen to her the way you would listen
    to your own daughter
    if she died too young
    and tried to speak to you
    across long distances.

Eurydice shakes out her umbrella.
She approaches the audience.
This time, she can speak.

EURYDICE. There was a roar, and a coldness –
    I think my husband was with me.
    What was my husband's name?

Eurydice turns to the stones.

    My husband's name? Do you know it?

The stones shrug their shoulders.

    How strange. I don't remember.
    It was horrible to see his face
    when I died. His eyes were
    two black birds
    and they flew to me.

    I said no – stay where you are –
    he needs you in order to see!

    When I got through the cold
    they made me swim in a river
    and I forgot his name.
    I forgot all the names.
    I know his name starts with my mouth
    shaped like a ball of twine –
    Oar – oar.
    I forget.

They took me to a tiny boat.
I only just fit inside.
I looked at the oars
and I wanted to cry.
I tried to cry but I just drooled a little.

I'll try now.

She tries to cry and finds that she can't.

EURYDICE. What happiness it would be to cry.

(She takes a breath.)

I was not lonely
only alone with myself
begging myself not to leave my own body
but I *was* leaving.

Good-bye, head – I said –
it inclined itself a little, as though to nod to me
in a solemn kind of way.

(She turns to the stones.)

How do you say good-bye to yourself?

They shake their heads.
A train whistle.
Eurydice steps onto a platform, surveying a large crowd.

EURYDICE. A train!

LITTLE STONE. The station is like a train but
there is no train.

BIG STONE. The train has wheels that are not wheels.

LOUD STONE. There is the opposite of a wheel and the
opposite of smoke and the opposite of a train.

A train pulls away.

EURYDICE. Oh! I'm waiting for someone to meet me, I
think.

Eurydice's Father approaches and takes her baggage.

FATHER. Eurydice.

EURYDICE. (*to the stones*) At last, a porter to meet me!
(*to the father*) Do you happen to know where the bank is? I need money. I've just arrived. I need to exchange my money at the Bureau de Change. I didn't bring traveler's checks because I left in such a hurry. They didn't even let me pack my suitcase. There's nothing in it! That's funny, right? Funny – ha ha! I suppose I can buy new clothes here. I would *really* love a bath.

FATHER. Eurydice!

EURYDICE. What is that language you're speaking? It gives me tingles. Say it again.

FATHER. Eurydice!

EURYDICE. Oooh – it's like a fruit! Again!

FATHER. Eurydice – I'm your father!

EURYDICE. (*strangely imitating*) Eurydice – I'm your father. How funny! You remind me of something but I can't understand a word you're saying. Say it again!

FATHER. Your father.

STONES. (*to the father*) Shut up, shut up!
She doesn't understand you.
She's dead now too.
You have to speak in the language of stones.

FATHER. You're dead now. I'm dead, too.

EURYDICE. Yes, that's right. I need a reservation. For the fancy hotel.

FATHER. When you were alive, I was your father.

STONES. Father is not a word that dead people understand.

BIG STONE. He is what we call subversive.

FATHER. When you were alive, I was your tree.

EURYDICE. My tree! Yes, the tall one in the back yard! I used to sit all day in its shade!

She sits at the feet of her father.

EURYDICE. Ah – there – shade!

LITTLE STONE. There is a problem here.

EURYDICE. Is there any entertainment at the hotel? Any dancing ladies? Like with the great big fans?

FATHER. I named you Eurydice. Your mother named all the other children. But Eurydice I chose for you.

BIG STONE. Be careful, sir.

FATHER. Eurydice. I wanted to remember your name. I asked the stones. They said: Forget the names – the names make you remember.

LOUD STONE. We told you how it works!

FATHER. One day it would not stop raining.

    I heard your name inside the rain – somewhere between the drops – I saw falling letters. Each letter of your name – I began to translate.

    E – I remembered elephants. U – I remembered ulcers and under. R – I remembered reindeers. I saw them putting their black noses into snow. Y – youth and yellow. D – dog, dig, daughter, day. Time poured into my head. The days of the week. Hours, months....

EURYDICE. The tree talks so beautifully.

STONES. Don't listen!

EURYDICE. I feel suddenly hungry! Where is the porter who met me at the station?

FATHER. Here I am.

EURYDICE. I would like a continental breakfast, please. Maybe some rolls and butter. Oh – and jam. Please take my suitcase to my room, if you would.

FATHER. I'm sorry, Miss, but there are no rooms here.

EURYDICE. What? No rooms? Where do people sleep?

FATHER. People don't sleep here.

EURYDICE. I have to say I'm very disappointed. It's been such a tiring day. I've been traveling all day – first on a river, then on an elevator that rained, then on a train...I thought someone would meet me at the station...

Eurydice is on the verge of tears.

STONES. Don't cry! Don't cry!

EURYDICE. I don't know where I am and there are all these
   stones and I hate them! They're horrible! I want a bath!
   I thought someone would meet me at the station!

FATHER. Don't be sad. I'll take your luggage to your room.

STONES. THERE ARE NO ROOMS!

He picks up her luggage.
He gives the stones a dirty look.
The sound of water in rusty pipes.

Scene 2

Orpheus writes a letter to Eurydice.

ORPHEUS. Dear Eurydice,

I miss you. No – that's not enough.

He crumples up the letter.
He writes a new letter.
He thinks.
He writes:

ORPHEUS. Dear Eurydice,

Symphony for twelve instruments.

(A pause.
He hears the music in his head.
He conducts.)

Love, Orpheus

He drops the letter as though into a mail slot.

Scene 3

The father creates a room out of string for Eurydice.

He makes four walls and a door out of string.
Time passes.
It takes time to build a room out of string.

Eurydice observes the underworld.
There isn't much to observe.
She plays hop-scotch without chalk.

Every so often,
the father looks at her,
happy to see her,
while he makes her room out of string.
She looks back at him, polite.

Scene 4

The father has completed the string room.
He gestures for Eurydice to enter.
She enters.

EURYDICE. Thank you. That will do.

She nods to her father.
He doesn't leave.

EURYDICE. Oh.

I suppose you want a tip.

He shakes his head.

EURYDICE. Would you run a bath for me?

FATHER. Yes, miss.

He exits the string room.
Eurydice opens her suitcase.
She is surprised that nothing is inside.
She sits down inside her suitcase.

Scene 5

ORPHEUS. Dear Eurydice,

I love you. I'm going to find you. I play the saddest music now that you're gone. You know I hate writing letters. I'll give this letter to a worm. I hope he finds you.

Love,

Orpheus

He drops the letter as though into a mail slot.

Scene 6

The father enters the string room with a letter on a silver tray.

FATHER. There is a letter for you, miss.

EURYDICE. A letter?

He nods.

FATHER. A letter.

He hands her the letter.

FATHER. It's addressed to you.

EURYDICE. There's dirt on it.

Eurydice wipes the dirt off the letter.
She opens it.
She scrutinizes it.
She does not know how to read it.
She puts it on the ground, takes off her shoes,
stands on the letter, and shuts her eyes.
She thinks, without language for the thought,
the melody: There's no place like home…

FATHER. Miss.

EURYDICE. What is it?

FATHER. Would you like me to *read* you the letter?

EURYDICE. "Read you the letter"?

FATHER. You can't do it with your feet.

(The father guides her off the letter, picks it up and begins to read.)

It's addressed to Eurydice. That's you.

EURYDICE. That's you.

FATHER. You.

It says: I love you.

EURYDICE. I love you?

FATHER. It's like your tree.

EURYDICE. Tall?

The father considers.

EURYDICE. Green?

FATHER. It's like sitting in the shade.

EURYDICE. Oh.

FATHER. It's like sitting in the shade with no clothes on.

EURYDICE. Oh! – yes.

FATHER. (*reading*) I'm going to find you. I play the saddest music –

EURYDICE. Music?

He whistles a note.

FATHER. It's like that.

She smiles.

EURYDICE. Go on.

FATHER. You know I hate writing letters. I'll give this letter to a worm. I hope he finds you.
Love,
Orpheus

EURYDICE. Orpheus?

FATHER. Orpheus.

A pause.

EURYDICE. That word!
It's like – I can't breathe.
Orpheus! My husband.

Eurydice looks at her father.
She recognizes him.

EURYDICE. Oh!

She embraces her father.

Scene 7

ORPHEUS. Dear Eurydice,

Last night I dreamed that we climbed Mount Olympus and we started to make love and all the strands of your hair were little faucets and water was streaming out of your head and I said, why is water coming out of your hair? And you said, gravity is very compelling.

And then we jumped off Mount Olympus and flew through the clouds and you held your knee to your chest because you skinned it on a sharp cloud and then we fell into a salty lake. Then I woke up and the window frightened me and I thought: Eurydice is dead. Then I thought – who is Eurydice? Then the whole room started to float and I thought: what are people? Then my bed clothes smiled at me with a crooked green mouth and I thought: who am I? It scares me, Eurydice. Please come back.

Love,
Orpheus

Scene 8

Eurydice and her Father in the string room.

FATHER. Did you get my letters?

EURYDICE. No! You wrote me letters?

FATHER. Every day.

EURYDICE. What did they say?

FATHER. Oh – nothing much. The usual stuff.

EURYDICE. Tell me the names of my mother and brothers and sisters.

FATHER. I don't think that's a good idea. It will make you sad.

EURYDICE. I want to know.

FATHER. It's a long time to be sad.

EURYDICE. I'd rather be sad.

THE STONES. Being sad is not allowed! Act like a stone.

Scene 9

Time shifts. Drops of water.
Eurydice and her father in the string room.

EURYDICE. Teach me another.

FATHER. Ostracize.

EURYDICE. What does it mean?

FATHER. To exclude. The Greeks decided who to banish. They wrote the name of the banished person on a white piece of pottery called ostrakon.

EURYDICE. Ostrakon.

Another.

FATHER. Peripatetic. From the Greek. It means to walk slowly, speaking of weighty matters, in bare feet.

EURYDICE. Peripatetic: a learned fruit, wandering through the snow.

Another.

FATHER. Defunct.

EURYDICE. Defunct.

FATHER. It means dead in a very abrupt way. Not the way I died, which was slowly. But all at once, in cowboy boots.

EURYDICE. Tell me a story of when you were little.

FATHER. Well, there was the time your uncle shot at me with a bee-bee gun and I was mad at him so I swallowed a nail.

Then there was the time I went to a dude ranch and I was riding a horse and I lassoed a car. The lady driving the car got out and spanked me. And your grandmother spanked me too.

EURYDICE. Remember the Christmas when she gave me a doll and I said, "If I see one more doll I'm going to throw up"?

FATHER. I think grammy was a little surprised when you said that.

EURYDICE. Tell me a story about your mother.

FATHER. The most vivid recollection I have of mother was seeing her at parties and in the house playing piano. When she was younger she was extremely animated. She could really play the piano. She could play everything by ear. They called her Flaming Sally.

EURYDICE. I never saw grammy play the piano.

FATHER. She was never the same after my father died. My father was a very gentle man.

EURYDICE. Tell me a story about your father.

FATHER. My father and I used to duck hunt. By the Mississippi River. He would call up old Frank the night before and ask, "Where are the ducks moving tonight?" Old Frank, he could really call the ducks.

It was hard for me to kill the poor little ducks, but you get caught up in the fervor of it. You'd get as many as ten ducks.

If you went over the limit – there were only so many ducks per person – father would throw the ducks to the side of the creek we were paddling on and make sure there was no game warden. If the warden was gone, he'd run back and get the extra ducks and throw them in the back of the car. My father was never a great conversationalist – but he loved to rhapsodize about hunting. He would always say, if I ever have to die, it's in a duck pond. And he did.

EURYDICE. There was something I always wanted to ask you. A story – or someone's name – I forget.

FATHER. Don't worry. You'll remember. There's plenty of time.

Scene 10

Orpheus writes a letter.

ORPHEUS. Dear Eurydice,

I wonder if you miss reading books in the under-world.

Orpheus holds the Collected Works of Shakespeare with a long string attached.
He drops it slowly to the ground.

Scene 11

Eurydice holds the Collected Works of Shakespeare.

EURYDICE. What is this?

She opens it. She doesn't understand it.
She throws the book on the ground.

EURYDICE. What are you?

She is wary of it, as though it might bite her.
She tries to understand the book.
She tries to make the book do something.

EURYDICE. (*to the book*) What do you do?

What do you DO?!

Say something!

I hate you!

She stands on the book, trying to read it.

EURYDICE. Damn you!

She throws the book.
She lies down in the string room.
Drops of water. Time passes.
The Father picks up the book.
He brushes it off.
In the string room,
the father teaches Eurydice how to read.
She looks over his shoulder as he reads out loud from
King Lear.

FATHER. We two alone will sing like birds in the cage.
When thou dost ask my blessing, I'll kneel down
And ask of thee forgiveness; so we'll live,
And pray and sing....

Scene 12

Orpheus, with a telephone.

ORPHEUS. For Eurydice – E, U, R, Y – that's right. No, there's no last name. It's not like that. What? No, I don't know the country. I don't know the city either. I don't know the street. I don't know – it probably starts with a vowel. Could you just – would you mind checking please – I would really appreciate it. You can't enter a name without a city? Why not? Well, thank you for trying. Wait – miss – it's a special case. She's dead. Well, thank you for trying. You have a nice day too.

He hangs up.

I'll find you. Don't move!

He fingers a glow-in-the-dark globe, looking for her.

Scene 13

Eurydice and her father in the string room.

EURYDICE. Tell me another story of when you were little.

FATHER. Well, there was my first piano recital. I was playing "I Got Rhythm". I played the first few chords and I couldn't remember the rest. I ran out of the room and locked myself in the bathroom.

EURYDICE. Then what happened?

FATHER. Your grandmother pulled me out of the bathroom and made me apologize to everyone in the auditorium. I never played piano after that. But I still know the first four chords – let's see –

(He plays the chords in the air with his hands)

Da Da *Dee* Da

Da Da *Dee* Da

Da Da *Dee* Da...

EURYDICE. What are the words?

FATHER. I can't remember.

Let's see...

Da da Dee Da

Da da Dee da...

They both start singing to the tune of I Got Rhythm.

FATHER & EURYDICE. Da da Dee Da

Da da Dee Da

Da da Dee Da

Da dee da da doo dee dee da.

Da da Da da

Da da Da da

Da Da da Da

Da da da...

Da da Dee Da

Da da dee da...

STONES. WHAT IS THAT NOISE?

LITTLE STONE. Stop singing!

LOUD STONE. STOP SINGING!

BIG STONE. Neither of you can carry a tune.

LITTLE STONE. It's awful.

STONES. DEAD PEOPLE CAN'T SING!

EURYDICE. I'm not a very good singer.

FATHER. Neither am I.

Scene 14

The Father leaves for work.
He takes his briefcase.
He waves to Eurydice.
She waves back.
She is alone in the string room.
She touches the string.

The Lord of the Underworld enters on his red tricycle.
Music from a heavy metal band accompanies his en-
trance.
His clothes and his hat are too small for him.
He stops pedaling at the entrance to the string room.

CHILD. Knock, knock.

EURYDICE. Who's there?

CHILD. I am Lord of the Underworld.

EURYDICE. Very funny.

CHILD. I am.

EURYDICE. Prove it.

CHILD. I can do chin-ups inside your bones. Close your
     eyes.

She closes her eyes.

EURYDICE. Ow.

CHILD. See?
     You're pretty.

EURYDICE. You're little.

CHILD. I grow downward. Like a turnip.

EURYDICE. What do you want?

CHILD. I wanted to see if you were comfortable.
     You're not itchy?

EURYDICE. No.

CHILD. That's good. Sometimes our residents get itchy.
     Then I scratch them.

EURYDICE. I'm not itchy.

CHILD. What's all this string?

EURYDICE. It's my room.

CHILD. Rooms are not allowed!

(To the stones.)

Tell her.

STONES. ROOMS ARE NOT ALLOWED!

CHILD. Who made your room?

EURYDICE. My father.

CHILD. Fathers are not allowed! Where is he?

EURYDICE. He's at work.

CHILD. We'll have to dip you in the river again and make sure you're good and dunked.

EURYDICE. Please, don't.

CHILD. Oooh – say that again. It's nice.

EURYDICE. Please, don't.

CHILD. Say it in my ear.

EURYDICE. *(towards his ear)* Please, don't.

CHILD. I like that.

(A seduction:)

I'll huff and I'll puff and I'll blow your house down!

(He blows on her face.)

I mean that in the nicest possible way.

EURYDICE. I have a husband.

CHILD. Husbands are for children. You need a lover. I'll be back.

(to the stones)

See that she's...comfortable.

STONES. We will!

CHILD. Good-bye.

EURYDICE. Good-bye.

STONES. Good-bye.

CHILD. I'm growing. Can you tell? I'm growing!

He laughs his hysterical laugh and speeds away on his red tricycle.

Scene 15

A big storm. The sound of rain on a roof.
Orpheus in a rain slicker.

ORPHEUS. (*shouting above the storm*) If a drop of water enters
the soil
at a particular angle, with a particular pitch,
what's to say a man can't ride one note
into the earth like a fireman's pole?

He puts a bucket on the ground to catch rain falling.
He looks at the rain falling into the bucket.
He tunes his guitar, trying to make the pitch of each note
correspond with the pitch of each water drop.

Orpheus wonders if one particular pitch
might lead him to the underworld.
Orpheus wonders if the pitch
he is searching for might
correspond to the pitch of a drop
of rain, as it enters the soil.
A pitch.

ORPHEUS. Eurydice – did you hear that?

Another pitch.

Eurydice? That's the note. That one, right there.

Scene 16

Eurydice and her father in the string room.

EURYDICE. Orpheus never liked words. He had his music. He would get a funny look on his face and I would say what are you thinking about and he would always be thinking about music.

If we were in a restaurant sometimes Orpheus would look sullen and wouldn't talk to me and I thought people felt sorry for me. I should have realized that women envied me. Their husbands talked too much.

But I wanted to talk to him about my notions. I was working on a new philosophical system. It involved hats.

This is what it is to love an artist: The moon is always rising above your house. The houses of your neighbors look dull and lacking in moonlight. But he is always going away from you. Inside his head there is always something more beautiful.

Orpheus said the mind is a slide ruler. It can fit around anything. Words can mean anything. Show me your body, he said. It only means one thing.

Scene 17

ORPHEUS. Eurydice!

Before I go down there, I won't practice my music. Some say practice. But practice is a word invented by cowards. The animals don't have a word for practice. A gazelle does not run for practice. He runs because he is scared or he is hungry. A bird doesn't sing for practice. She sings because she's happy or sad. So I say: store it up. The music sounds better in my head than it does in the world. When songs are pressing against my throat, then, only then, I will go down and sing for the devils and they will cry through their parched throats.

Eurydice, don't kiss a dead man. Their lips look red and tempting but put your tongue in their mouths and it tastes like oatmeal. I know how much you hate oatmeal.

I'm going the way of death.

Here is my plan: Tonight, when I go to bed, I will turn off the light and put a straw in my mouth. When I fall asleep, I will crawl through the straw and my breath will push me like a great wind into the darkness and I will sing your name and I will arrive. I have consulted the almanacs, the footstools, and the architects, and everyone agrees: I found the right note. Wait for me.

Love,

Orpheus

Scene 18

EURYDICE. I got a letter. From Orpheus.

FATHER. What did he say?

EURYDICE. He says he's going to come find me.

FATHER. How?

EURYDICE. He's going to sing.

Scene 19

Darkness.
An unearthly light surrounds Orpheus.
He holds a straw up to his lips in slow motion.

He blows into the straw.

The sound of breath.
He disappears.

Scene 20

The sound of a knock.

LITTLE STONE. Someone is knocking!

BIG STONE. Who is it?

LOUD STONE. Who is it?

The sound of three loud knocks, insistent.

STONES. NO ONE KNOCKS AT THE DOOR OF THE DEAD!

THIRD MOVEMENT

Scene 1

Orpheus stands at the gates of hell.
He opens his mouth.

He looks like he's singing, but he's silent.
Music surrounds him.
The melody Orpheus hummed in the first scene,
repeated over and over again.

Raspberries, peaches and plums drop from the ceiling
into the River. Perhaps only in our imagination.
Orpheus keeps singing.

The stones weep.
They look at their tears, bewildered.
Orpheus keeps singing.

A child comes out of a trap door.

CHILD. Who are you?

ORPHEUS. I am Orpheus.

CHILD. I am lord of the underworld.

ORPHEUS. But you're so young!

CHILD. Don't be rude.

ORPHEUS. Sorry.

Did you like my music?

CHILD. No. I prefer happy music with a nice beat.

ORPHEUS. Oh.

CHILD. You've come for Eurydice.

ORPHEUS. Yes!

CHILD. And you thought singing would get you through
the gates of hell.

ORPHEUS. See here. I want my wife.

What do I have to do?

CHILD. You'll have to do more than sing.

ORPHEUS. I'm not sure what you mean, sir.

CHILD. Start walking home. Your wife just might be on the road behind you. We make it real nice here. So people want to stick around. As you walk, keep your eyes facing front. If you look back at her – poof! She's gone.

ORPHEUS. I can't look at her?

CHILD. No.

ORPHEUS. Why?

CHILD. Because.

ORPHEUS. Because?

CHILD. Because!

ORPHEUS. I look straight ahead. That's all?

CHILD. Yes.

ORPHEUS. That's easy.

CHILD. Good.

The child smiles. He exits.

Scene 2

Eurydice and her father.

EURYDICE. I hear him at the gates! That's his music!
He's come to save me!

FATHER. Do you want to go with him?

EURYDICE. Yes, of course!

She sees that his face falls a little.

EURYDICE. Oh – you'll be lonely, won't you?

FATHER. No, no. You should go to your husband. You
should have grandchildren. You'll all come down and
meet me one day.

EURYDICE. Are you sure?

FATHER. You should love your family until the grapes grow
dust on their purple faces.
I'll take you to him.

EURYDICE. Now?

FATHER. It's for the best.

He takes her arm.
They process, arm in arm, as at a wedding.
Wedding music.
They are solemn and glad.
They walk.
They see Orpheus up ahead.

FATHER. Is that him?

EURYDICE. Yes – I think so –

FATHER. His shoulders aren't very broad. Can he take care
of you?

Eurydice nods.

FATHER. Are you sure?

EURYDICE. Yes.

FATHER. There's one thing you need to know. If he turns
around and sees you, you'll die a second death. Those
are the rules. So step quietly. And don't cry out.

EURYDICE. I won't.

FATHER. Good-bye.

They embrace.

EURYDICE. I'll come back to you. I seem to keep dying.

FATHER. Don't let them dip you in the River too long, the second time. Hold your breath.

EURYDICE. I'll look for a tree.

FATHER. I'll write you letters.

EURYDICE. Where will I find them?

FATHER. I don't know yet. I'll think of something. Good-bye, Eurydice.

EURYDICE. Good-bye.

They move away.
The father waves.
She waves back,
as though on an old steamer ship.
The father exits.
Eurydice takes a deep breath. She takes a big step forward towards the audience, on an unseen gangplank
She is brave.
She takes another step forward.
She hesitates.
She is all of a sudden not so brave.
She is afraid.
SHE LOOKS BACK.
She turns in the direction of her father, her back to the audience. He's out of sight.

EURYDICE. Wait, come back!

LITTLE STONE. You can't go back now, Eurydice.

LOUD STONE. Face forward!

BIG STONE. Keep walking.

EURYDICE. I'm afraid!

LOUD STONE. Your husband is waiting for you, Eurydice.

EURYDICE. I don't recognize him! That's a stranger!

LITTLE STONE. Go on. It's him.

EURYDICE. I want to go home! I want my father!

LOUD STONE. You're all grown up now. You have a husband.

STONES. TURN AROUND!

EURYDICE. Why?

STONES. BECAUSE!

EURYDICE. That's a stupid reason.

LITTLE STONE. Orpheus braved the gates of hell
    to find you.

LOUD STONE. He played the saddest music.

BIG STONE. Even we –

STONES. The stones –

LITTLE STONE. cried when we heard it.

She turns slowly, facing front.

EURYDICE. That's Orpheus?

STONES. Yes, that's him!

EURYDICE. Where's his music?

STONES. It's in your head.

*Orpheus walks slowly, in a straight line, with the focus
of a tight-rope walker.
Eurydice moves to follow him.
She follows him, several steps behind.
THEY WALK.
Eurydice follows him with precision, one step for every
step he takes.
She makes a decision.
She increases her pace.
She takes two steps for every step that Orpheus takes. She
catches up to him.*

EURYDICE. Orpheus?

*HE TURNS TOWARDS HER, STARTLED.
ORPHEUS LOOKS AT EURYDICE.
EURYDICE LOOKS AT ORPHEUS.
THE WORLD FALLS AWAY.*

ORPHEUS. You startled me.

> *A small sound – ping.*
> *They turn their faces away from each other,*
> *matter-of-fact, compelled.*
> *The lights turn blue.*

EURYDICE. I'm sorry.

ORPHEUS. Why?

EURYDICE. I don't know.

ORPHEUS. (*syncopated*)	**EURYDICE.**
You always clapped your hands	I could never spell the word
on the third beat	rhythm –
you couldn't wait for the fourth.	it is such a difficult
Remember –	word to spell –
I tried to teach you –	r – y – no – there's an H in it –
you were always one step ahead	somewhere – a breath –
of the music	
your sense of rhythm –	rhy – rhy –
it was – off –	rhy –

ORPHEUS. I would say clap on the down-beat –
no, the down-beat –
It's dangerous not
to have a sense of rhythm.
You LOSE things when you can't
keep a simple beat –
why'd you have to say my name –
Eurydice –

EURYDICE. I'm sorry.

ORPHEUS. I know we used to fight –
it seems so silly now – if –

EURYDICE. If ifs and ands were pots and pans
there'd be no need for tinkers –

ORPHEUS. Why?

They begin walking away from each other
on extensive unseen boardwalks,
their figures long shadows,
looking straight ahead.

EURYDICE. If ifs and ands were pots and pans
    there'd be no need for tinkers –

ORPHEUS. Eurydice –

EURYDICE. I think I see the gates.
    The stones – the boat –
    it looks familiar –
    the stones look happy to see me –

ORPHEUS. Don't look –

EURYDICE. Wow! That's the happiest I've ever seen them!

ORPHEUS. (*syncopated*)	**EURYDICE.**
Think of things we did:	Everything is so grey –
	it looks familiar –
we went ice skating –	like home –
	our house was –
I wore a red sweater –	grey – with a red door –
	we had two cats
	and two dogs
	and two fish
	that died –

ORPHEUS. Will you talk to me!

EURYDICE. The train looks like
    the opposite of a train –

ORPHEUS. Eurydice!
    WE'VE KNOWN EACH OTHER FOR CENTURIES!
    I want to reminisce!
    Remember when you wanted your name in a song
    so I put your name in a song –
    When I played my music
    at the gates of hell
    I was singing your name
    over and over and over again.

Eurydice.

He grows quiet.
They walk away from each other on extended lines until
they are out of sight.

Scene 3

THE STONES. Finally.

 Some peace.

LOUD STONE. And quiet.

THE STONES. Like the old days.

 No music.

 No conversation.

 How about that.

 A pause.

FATHER. With Eurydice gone it will be a second death for me.

LITTLE STONE. Oh, please, sir –

BIG STONE. We're tired.

FATHER. Do you understand the love a father has for his daughter?

LITTLE STONE. Love is a big, funny word.

BIG STONE. Dead people should be seen and not heard.

 The father looks at the stones.
 He looks at the string room.
 He dismantles the string room,
 matter-of-fact.
 There's nothing else to do.
 This can take time.
 It takes time to dismantle a room made of string.
 Music.
 He sits down in what used to be the string room.

FATHER. How does a person remember to forget.

 It's difficult.

LOUD STONE. It's not difficult.

LITTLE STONE. We told you how it works.

LOUD STONE. Dip yourself in the river.

BIG STONE. Dip yourself in the river.

LITTLE STONE. Dip yourself in the river.

FATHER. I need directions.

LOUD STONE. That's ridiculous.

BIG STONE. There are no directions.

A pause.
The father thinks.

FATHER. I remember.
Take Tri-State South – 294 –
to Route 88 West.
Take Route 88 West to Route 80.
You'll go over a bridge.
Go three miles and you'll come
to the exit for Middle Road.
Proceed 3 to 4 miles.
Duck Creek Park will be on the right.
Take a left on Fernwood Avenue.

Continue straight on Fernwood past
two intersections.
Fernwood will curve to the right leading
you to Forest Road.
Take a left on Forest Road.
Go two blocks.
Pass the first entrance to the alley on the right.
Take the second entrance.
You'll go about 100 yards.
A red brick house will
be on the right.
Look for Illinois license plates.
Go inside the house.

In the living room,
look out the window.
You'll see the lights on the Mississippi River.
Take off your shoes.
Walk down the hill.
You'll pass a tree good for climbing on the right.

Cross the road.
Watch for traffic.
Cross the train tracks.
Catfish are sleeping in the mud, on your left.
Roll up your jeans.
Count to ten.
Put your feet in the river
and swim.

He dips himself in the river.
A small metallic sound of forgetfulness – ping.
The sound of water.
He lies down on the ground,
curled up, asleep.

Eurydice returns and sees that her string room is gone.

EURYDICE. Where's my room?

The stones are silent.

EURYDICE. (*to the stones*) WHERE IS MY ROOM?
Answer me!

LITTLE STONE. It's none of our business.

LOUD STONE. What are you doing here?

BIG STONE. You should be with your husband.

LOUD STONE. Up there.

EURYDICE. Where's my father?

The stones point to the father.

EURYDICE. (*To the stones*) Why is he sleeping?

The stones shrug their shoulders.

EURYDICE. (*to her father*) I've come back!

LOUD STONE. He can't hear you.

LITTLE STONE. It's too late.

EURYDICE. What are you talking about?

BIG STONE. He dipped himself in the River.

EURYDICE. My father did not dip himself in the River.

STONES. He did!

We saw him!

LOUD STONE. He wanted some peace and quiet.

EURYDICE. (*to the stones*) HE DID NOT!.

(to her father)

Listen. I'll teach you the words. Then we'll know each other again. Ready? We'll start with my name. Eurydice. E U R Y ....

BIG STONE. He can't hear you.

LOUD STONE. He can't see you.

LITTLE STONE. He can't remember you.

EURYDICE. (*to the stones*) I hate you! I've always hated you! Shut up! Shut up! Shut up!

(to her father)

Listen. I'll tell you a story.

LITTLE STONE. Try speaking in the language of stones.

LOUD STONE. It's a very quiet language.

Like if the pores in your

face opened up and wanted to talk.

EURYDICE. Stone.

Rock.

Tree. Rock. Stone.

It doesn't work.
She holds her father.

LOUD STONE. Didn't you already mourn for your father, young lady?

LITTLE STONE. Some things should be left well enough alone.

BIG STONE. To mourn twice is excessive.

LITTLE STONE. To mourn three times a sin.

LOUD STONE. Life is like a good meal.

BIG STONE. Only gluttons want more food when they finish their helping.

LITTLE STONE. Learn to be more moderate.

BIG STONE. It's weird for a dead person to be morbid.

LITTLE STONE. We don't like to watch it!

LOUD STONE. We don't like to see it!

BIG STONE. It makes me uncomfortable.

Eurydice cries.

STONES. Don't cry!

Don't cry!

BIG STONE. Learn the art of keeping busy!

EURYDICE. IT'S HARD TO KEEP BUSY WHEN YOU'RE DEAD!

STONES. It is not hard!

We keep busy

and we like it

We're busy busy busy stones

Watch us work

Keeping still

Keeping quiet

It's hard work

to be a stone

No time for crying

No no no!

EURYDICE. I HATE YOU! I'VE ALWAYS HATED YOU!

She runs towards them and tries to hit them.

STONES. Go ahead.

Try to hit us.

LITTLE STONE. You'll hurt your fist.

BIG STONE. You'll break your hand.

STONES. Ha ha ha!

Enter the child.
He has grown.
He is now at least ten feet tall.
His voice sounds suspiciously
like the nasty interesting man's.

CHILD. Is there a problem here?

STONES. No, sir.

CHILD. (*to Eurydice*) You chose to stay with us, huh? Good.

(He looks her over.)

Perhaps to be my bride?

EURYDICE. I told you. You're too young.

CHILD. I'll be the judge of that.

I've grown.

EURYDICE. Yes – I see that.

CHILD. I'm ready to be a man now. I'm ready – to be – a man.

EURYDICE. Please. Leave me alone.

CHILD. I'll have them start preparing the satins and silks. You can't refuse me. I've made my choice.

EURYDICE. Can I have a moment to prepare myself?

CHILD. Don't be long. The wedding songs are already being written. They're very quiet. Inaudible, you might say. A dirt-filled orchestra for my bride. Don't trouble the songs with your music, I say. A song is two dead bodies rubbing under the covers to keep warm.

He exits.

STONES. Well, well, well!

LITTLE STONE. You had better prepare yourself.

EURYDICE. There is nothing to prepare.

BIG STONE. You had better comb your hair.

LOUD STONE. You had better find a veil.

EURYDICE. I don't need a veil. I need a pen!

LITTLE STONE. Pens are forbidden here.

EURYDICE. I need a pencil then.

LOUD STONE. Pencils, too.

EURYDICE. Damn you! I'll dip you in the river!

BIG STONE. Too late, too late!

EURYDICE. There must be a pen. There are. There must be.

*She remembers the pen and paper in the breast pocket of
her father's coat.*
She takes them out.
She holds the pen up to show the stones.

EURYDICE. A pen.

She writes a letter.

EURYDICE. Dear Orpheus,

I'm sorry. I don't know what came over me. I was
afraid. I'm not worthy of you. But I still love you, I
think. Don't try to find me again. You would be lonely
for music. I want you to be happy. I want you to marry
again. I am going to write out instructions for your
next wife.

To my Husband's Next Wife:

Be gentle.

Be sure to comb his hair when it's wet.

Do not fail to notice

that his face flushes pink

like a bride's

when you kiss him.

Give him lots to eat.

He forgets to eat and he gets cranky.

When he's sad,

kiss his forehead and I will thank you.

Because he is a young prince

and his robes are too heavy on him.

His crown falls down

around his ears.

I'll give this letter to a worm. I hope he finds you.

Love,

Eurydice.

She puts the letter on the ground.

She dips herself in the river.
A small metallic sound of forgetfulness – ping.
The sound of water.
She lies down next to her father, as though asleep.

The sound of an elevator – ding.
Orpheus appears in the elevator.
He sees Eurydice.
He is happy.
The elevator starts raining on Orpheus.
He forgets.
He steps out of the elevator.

He sees the letter on the ground.
He picks it up.
He scrutinizes it.
He can't read it.
He stands on it.
He closes his eyes.
The sound of water.
Then silence.

The end.

OTHER TITLES AVAILABLE FROM SAMUEL FRENCH

THE CLEAN HOUSE

Sarah Ruhl
2005 Pulitzer Prize Finalist

This extraordinary new play by an exciting new voice in the American drama was runner-up for the Pulitzer Prize. The play takes place in what the author describes as "metaphysical Connecticut", mostly in the home of a married couple who are both doctors. They have hired a housekeeper named Matilde, an aspiring comedian from Brazil who's more interested in coming up with the perfect joke than in house-cleaning. Lane, the lady of the house, has an eccentric sister named Virginia who's just nuts about house-cleaning. She and Matilde become fast friends, and Virginia takes over the cleaning while Matilde works on her jokes. Trouble comes when Lane's husband Charles reveals that he has found his soul mate, or "bashert" in a cancer patient named Anna, on whom he has operated. The actors who play Charles and Anna also play Matilde's parents in a series of dream-like memories, as we learn the story about how they literally killed each other with laughter, giving new meaning to the phrase, "I almost died laughing." This theatrical and wildly funny play is a whimsical and poignant look at class, comedy and the true nature of love. 1m, 4f (#6266)

"Fresh, funny ... a memorable play, imbued with a somehow comforting philosophy: that the messes and disappointments of life are as much a part of its beauty as romantic love and chocolate ice cream, and a perfect punch line can be as sublime as the most wrenchingly lovely aria." — NY Times